THIS BOOK BELONGS TO

~~Kiwi~~   ~~Pearl~~

Mia
....

....

LADYBIRD BOOKS

UK | USA | Canada | Ireland | Australia | India | New Zealand | South Africa

Ladybird Books is part of the Penguin Random House group of companies
whose addresses can be found at global.penguinrandomhouse.com.

www.penguin.co.uk   www.puffin.co.uk   www.ladybird.co.uk

 Penguin
Random House
UK

First published in Australia by Puffin Books, 2021

This edition published in Great Britain by Ladybird Books Ltd, 2022
001

Text and illustrations copyright © Ludo Studio Pty Ltd, 2021

 LU DO   **BBC STUDIOS**

Printed in Italy

The authorized representative in the EEA is Penguin Random House Ireland,
Morrison Chambers, 32 Nassau Street, Dublin D02 YH68

A CIP catalogue record for this book is available from the British Library

ISBN: 978-0-241-55187-5

All correspondence to:
Ladybird Books, Penguin Random House Children's
One Embassy Gardens, 8 Viaduct Gardens, London SW11 7BW

 FSC
www.fsc.org

MIX
Paper from
responsible sources
FSC® C018179

BLUEY

CAMPING

The Heelers are on a camping trip. Bluey wants to build a stick house with Bingo, but Mum has other plans.
"Bingo's coming with me," Mum says. "She hasn't had a bath in **three days!**"
So, off Bluey goes to the creek, alone.

As Bluey searches for sticks, she hears a voice.
"Bonjour."

"Hi! My name's Bluey."
"Salut, Bluey. *Je suis* Jean Luc."

Bluey doesn't understand what Jean Luc is saying, but that doesn't stop them building a stick house together.

OH! C'EST TRÈS BEAU.

"Now we need some food to eat," says Bluey.

"We can plant this seed, like farmers! This will grow into a big tree with fruit on it."

"But it might take a while," she adds. "And we need something to eat *now*."

Suddenly, they hear a **howl** coming through the forest.

"Hide!" shouts Bluey.

SNUFF, SNUFFLE, SNORT!

"It's a wild pig," Bluey says. "*Sanglier*!" says Jean Luc.

Bluey and Jean Luc make a plan to capture the wild pig, but . . .

He escapes!

Never mind.

"Bluey, dinner!" Mum calls.
Then Jean Luc's dad calls to him. "Jean Luc, *dîner*!"

"See you tomorrow!" Bluey
says. They both run off
to their families.

GOODNIGHT.

The next morning,
Bluey and Jean Luc
are ready to play.

JEAN LUC!

BONJOUR!

"Hmm, no fruit tree yet.
We need a better plan
to catch that wild pig,
or we'll have no food for
the winter!"

"I've got an idea," Bluey tells Jean Luc.
"My dad taught me how to do this."

WILD PIG RUNS away.

BLUEY SCARES
WILD PIG.

Jean LUC JUMPS OUT.

HOORAY!

They wait until they hear the wild pig
roar, and then . . .

It's time to head back to camp for the night.
"Goodbye, Jean Luc," says Bluey happily. "See you tomorrow."

"*Non*, Bluey," Jean Luc calls.
"*Au revoir!*"

The next morning, Bluey discovers that the seed they planted is growing into a little tree.

JEAN LUC! COME QUICKLY! JEAN LUC!

But she can't see Jean Luc anywhere. Not at his campsite . . .

or at their stick house.

Bluey runs back to Mum, who tells her that Jean Luc must have left. His holiday is over.

"What?!" says Bluey. "You mean they're gone?"

That night, while Bingo has a bush wee,
Bluey asks Mum why Jean Luc had to leave.

"Sometimes, special people come into our lives,
stay for a bit, and then they have to go," says Mum.

"But that's sad," says Bluey.

"It is," says Mum. "But the bit where they were here was happy, wasn't it?"

"Yeah. We caught a wild pig together!" Bluey says.

"Maybe that makes it all worth it," says Mum.

"Will I ever see him again?"
asks Bluey.
"Well, you never know,"
says Mum.